David + Karen —

In Friendship —

[signature]

THE
MYSTIC DANCE

LORENZO LAGO

The Mystic Dance by Lorenzo Lago
Copyright 2019

Back Cover Photo: Marissa Todd, www.marissatoddphotography.com

Correspondence: www.lorenzolago.com

ISBN# 9781095581735

THE MYSTIC DANCE

Dedicated to those that share the same gaze.

Lorenzo Lago
2019

TABLE OF CONTENTS

AUTHOR'S NOTE

As requested, I have blended new and previously published verse to complete my fifth manuscript, *The Mystic Dance.* The book is a collection of sensual and sentimental prose that appear in my four books, *Romance On The High Seas, Journey, The Fire*, and *In the Light of the Jungle Moon.*

This request to assemble my passionate prose is a joy for me as I consider to be swept away in the allure, the fascination and the caress of romance is to feel alive!

SUMMER

Nature's kiss and your scented skin
   sunburned in roses of passion
      such the nourishing taste
         so naked and mischievous

SPELLBOUND

A standing ovation for the way you enter
thundering beauty in heels
    swaying confidence
    oh, your roaring presence!

How well you present yourself
such flare
classic, like colleagues of seasons merging within the eternal

I'm smitten
I want to taste you, all of you
You are earth
    its strength, its essence
        and its exotic

Earth's jewels shine in delight and adorn your body

I do so savor this golden harvest
I immerse myself within the bounty

Passion's equation solved so easily

SAVAGE ROSE

Of course it would grow here
gracefully, in sun or shade
in splendor and in sin
this lush flower of romance
exotic blossom of enchantment

I so savor this mystic scent!
so sweet of fragrance

The hypnotic dance you turn
exposing a sacred rhythm
this fierce cadence floods our senses

How well you've created your web
    you so silk, and me, so spun!

PHOTO, A THOUSAND MILES AWAY

I carry your photo with me
kept within my journal of poetry in progress

I can be on the other side of the world
riding waves on a lost island
resting in the shade
a cool drink in hand
and there is that look on your face

I took this photo after we made love
I'd like to share it with others
I would like to boast
but I don't
I respect how free you are with me
how you thrill in the wild war of making love
and how you rejoice in what we share

I see it on your face in this photo
you have got the power
you know I am thinking about you and your body
all wrapped around me
right now
on the other side of the world
a thousand miles away

ROCK AND ROLL TONIGHT

the suspense of your arrival
moments
    till you are deep within my arms
moments
    till we both surrender

the grand anticipation of seeing you
    come through the door
your body dancing as you walk inside my space

naked, you are radiant
like nothing I have ever seen
your whispers sing sinfully
your scent so sweet
like the scent of plumeria,
    gardenia
or a dark red rose
    a red that is almost black

my Venus
tonight we will awaken, soothe and share our senses
tonight we will caress, compliment and celebrate
tonight we ignite the spirit with dazzling romance

A FRENCH DECEMBER

"Paris isn't for changing planes", declares a stylish Audrey Hepburn
"Paris is for lovers", replies a woeful Humphrey Bogart

> *Dialogue from Sabrina, the 1954 motion picture from Paramount Pictures*

You suggest we reunite in Paris, and proclaim we will love it!
    Yes, my French Muse, your declaration rang true, we so love it!

Our Montmartre hotel oozes with ambiance
espresso each morning at the street-side cafe
In French fashion,
    we besiege ourselves feasting on extravagant cuisine,
        drinking smoky burgundy
            all snuggles and cuddles

Starving to share our passion,
    we become ravenous and make love all day, and all night

It is mad loving!
        not tidy like a grand garden
    not brushed gentle by a scented breeze
        but unkempt
            daring wild love

We saturate our souls in sinful sweetness
    exposing all the lavish layers
        we are run ragged by savage love

Unleashing centuries of captivating fury, our reuniting is a tour de force

ACROSS THE THRESHOLD

This is some kind of home run
one of those homers that skyrocket out of the park
    "POW, OUTA OF HERE!"

I love our honeymoon
our romance poised in stanzas of velvet and silk
the vivid hues braided so intimately within our sunrise and our setting sun

Lover, I want you to be naughty
    as naughty and wicked as you wish
let all your mischievous daydreams emerge
    and don't delay
        fantasies are safe with me
            for I treasure your hidden desires

I love to see the savage within you erupt and cover me in reckless sin!

WE CELEBRATE MY FAVORITE TIME

there is romance
when we never want it to end
nights of love don't stop in the morning
daybreak just puts more light and beauty on your body

we kiss as morning warmth
slices the cool air away
we find ourselves within the lure of soothing passion

together we know this is perfect

I can hear your whispers
and calling for more
I can smell the love of your body
I admire your absolute pose
we are so close
we are breathing in each other's soul

your time has arrived
you can not stop what is coming next
this moment of ecstasy
this is my favorite time
you are every part of this space
you lose yourself and you find yourself
you are complete
you are every woman
right now giving and taking
you are pure
correct
savage
all that is graceful on earth

MYSTERIOUS

spill words upon an empty page

fill the space with erotic rage

laughter, a moan, beauty sewn

THE NYMPHS ARE BECKONING

Hylas is not the only man that abandoned his ship
   to be awoken by your charm

The ardent exploits, the violent storms and victorious battles
   all in vain
   forsaken by the allure of your invitation

Sorcerous of my words
I have traveled such a noble distance to behold your treasure

Beauty, Grace, Favor the Daughters of Jupiter
     Immortal Goddesses of Charm
       pull me into your pool of splendor
        drown me within your wonder
          seize me forever within the volume of your mythical grasp
           your gift is to bathe within the bliss you possess

Your song summons
I must compose exalted verses proclaiming the depth of your glory

GOLDEN ARROW

myth has it that Cupid's mother was Venus
the Goddess of Love
Cupid's father was Mars
the God of War

so Cupid is cunning, and he is a troublemaker
he has this duality of love and war
Cupid shoots golden arrows so one will fall in love
and lead arrows so one will fall out of love

in the past I have been to battle
I armed myself with the defenses of questions, flowers and emotions
and still arrows of gold and lead slipped within my spirit

my sweet empress
one of Cupid's flaming golden arrows has pierced my skin
this arrow has driven deep into my heart
and deeper into my soul

this is a profound wound
I am bleeding emotions that I have never felt
I am oozing with love's infectious symptoms
my fever is great, and I don't want it to stop
I am delirious with visions of you

at first your stark beauty simply overwhelmed me
now my infatuation has become insatiable

dark empress, you prowl within the forest of my world
your turquoise necklace rests in the clearing of your breasts

from the darkest night ever
you were born to the river of your soul
you travel on my map marked unknown

I am not lost in this darkness
I am found

the buried treasure of true spirit
expands its wings
fascinated and free
flight

MUSE

Daughter of Neptune
    convincing is the storm of your mermaid soul
    fragrant is your feast, your salty bounty

Daughter of the Haunted Evening
    nymph of light and dark eternal
    the twilight of your convincing tonic
    life's eternal mystery unraveled with one sweet sip

Attractive is the dance you turn
    yours is an indulgent swoon
        charmed, like heaven's river

My craving rewarded by the grasp of this secret thread
so rich in tenderness, its echo resonates truth
liberating seasons of naked poetry

Convincing femme, the sunrise gathers at your lips
you have awoken the song of a rousing heart
my vision is released, my inspiration unleashed!

I submerse myself in your mermaid water
    I besiege myself in your forest laughter

Only to become
      a beast and barbarian
          a man of honor
             the legendary king

ISLAND MAGIC

this is a French island
each day fragrant flowers decorate the tables and bar
we wear some of these small flowers behind our ears
we are dining on lush local fruit and fresh tuna
we are drinking rich red wine
and strong espresso

local young women sit in shallow water
their small bathing suits fit comfortably
on the sandy bottom
with bare breasts
dark brown skin
long black hair
they inspire artists to make them unforgettable
and who could forget them

this a grand time of our relationship
we are in the habit of kissing
  at least two dozen times every hour
people near us think we are newlyweds

I can not get enough of you
and thankfully
you can't seem to get enough

so we lock ourselves away from everyone
for long periods of time
we still get plenty of sun
we bathe in the blue lagoon
but we can not help ourselves
we are intimate and excessive

I like the way you are in this heat
what has gotten into you
in this sensual sauna you lose all and any apprehension
you seem to be living out your fantasies here
the woman within you has become a seductive animal
you make love to me, sleep, make love, sleep
and love again

sweetheart, are you trying to wear me out
this is the way I like it
please keep trying

YOU WEAR IT SO WELL

From the ocean, she rises
    splendor gathers at her feet
        fascination encircles her body

Venus of creation
I'm always amazed how you enter a room
it takes my breath away

      Long is your slender figure sipping the evening twilight
Stunning, dressed in your sheer silk, you flow like a summer breeze
    And when you undress, and oh so skillfully,
        the breeze heightens and a blustery wind transpires and runs amok
            I love it so!

I can't wait to whisper lavish words upon you
    to envelop my arms about you
        unfold your sensual silk and velvet
            weave your textured charm about me
                cultivate the thrill that makes this so memorable

Your ghost is for all poets

LOVE SONG

Sweetened by sea and salt
   woven in sand and thunder
      lingering for years of nights
The sharpened blue edge of glass is persuaded,
 and softens to a tender touch
     tossed smooth and legendary
       becoming the birth of a calming stone
         polished, and absorbed

This night mist of emotions that our breath shares
Adrift, floating out to sea
   bound by a caressing brush
     flush with a harvest of mystery

Only together among rivers and skies
Colored with your scarlet blood kisses
   we will fly
   soaring with grace through shadows
     through light
Scattering the night with a rosebush of whispers
       truths and twilight promises

An April spring gathers at your mouth
There, I am caressed
    inflaming a sweetened life

Oh My Salted Mermaid
    My Infinite
    This exploration has now brought me to the tender truth

Passion's warm waves roll over my senses
Moist with the abyss of love's morning
    as the pagan dew envelops the expanse of your skin and scent
        fragrant with dusk and dawn

As the rose becomes the love song for our season

THE STORM OF YOU

Your phantom presence raging within my soul
thundering amid the cliffs of self
so drenched in emotion,
    I claw my way to the pinnacle of your existence

I see that this is how one reinvents oneself
this is how I replenish my world

Can you hear my heartbeat?

LOVE POEM FROM FRANCE

The Louvre Museum in Paris contains an amazing assemblage of art and artifacts. The museum's impressive collection of antiquities is too much for you and I to digest this morning, and vowing that we will return, we elect to make a swift departure from the museum.

Stepping into the crisp winter air, we stroll hand in hand through the Paris morning. Entering a quiet borough, we stop at a street side café and order rich coffee and croissants. Glancing through our notes, and surveying the sites to explore today, we discover that we are in close vicinity to Rodin Museum with is the residence that retains many of Rodin's pieces.

Upon our entrée into the picturesque chateau, we are charmed by such a refined display of Auguste Rodin sculptures, paintings and drawings. Adding to our visit, rays of warm sunshine penetrate through the museum's wealth of windows creating a haunted illumination upon each piece.

We approach the infamous sculpture, The Kiss. This celebrated marble carving is of a man and woman embracing. The two are joined together by a kiss, an eternal kiss. The passionate connection they share appears everlastingly.

I glance at you as you study the sculpture. The afternoon sun bathes a hypnotic glow over the marble and your sleek figure and your stirring profile. As radiant beams of sun creep through the room, you complete this theater of art. I don't think Rodin could have composed anything as stunning as you. My love, you appear so beautiful!

FINALLY, HERE IN BED!

early evening
I'm staring at your lips
beauties
spectacular, yes!
and meant to be kissed!

the intoxicating scent of your body
igniting my imagination
romance and animal
rapture

dancing
touching
our arms
around
we are moving
    into this loving
wonderfully
no stopping us now!

this lagoon of your youthful,
    eternal splendor
this shimmering expanse
    of your beauty
the lure and woo of an angel
and my thirst
    for a new landscape

this thrill of a new wind
    glorious and persuading
        convincing
easily
    my heart opens
    to heaven on earth

sweetest of sweet candy
    you are playing with me
I have to laugh at myself
    as I lose myself

I soar across the water of your presence

dancing
touching
our arms
around
we are moving
    into this loving
wonderfully
no stopping us now!

SUMMER FIRE

summer kiss the night
sky blanket
    deep blue
        to black
the long night
sharing
   exploring you
      loving you

naked
your arms
   your long fingers
stretched
   in poetic pose

tonight
I've been
   everywhere
      within your body and soul
I feel saturated with
   the pure woman that you are

wrapped in each other's arms
our growing warmth
a world of smoldering desires
this heat could start a forest fire

stretching for miles
    uncontainable
        inexhaustible
heaven and hell all in flames

we did not want to stop
our senses
    burned to the ground
        to the earth
            to the beginning

BEAUTY

a straw-hat breeze pushed you into my arms
the siren's trance of a healing woman
thank you sweetheart
you swept away all memories of betrayal and loneliness
drama and damage perished forever
I wandered for eternities in search of a stirring femme
we found each other with a simple glance
together, all the alluring senses have come alive
we travel on an ignited avenue of craving
ravishing each other with steamy kisses
seizing one another's body like there is no tomorrow!

ah, tonight's rising moon fascination
creative moonlight
mischievous midnight
delightful, delicious, hypnotic
souls together snuggle and spoon
such a persuading caress
silky sacrifice of clothing
skin to skin
my wild jewel
roll your love over on top of me!

I welcome this sexy dream
splash your wicked sins on me
addictive, pleading scent of desire
magically, you sigh, smile and sway
dance your taboo over my life
your samba has me ablaze!

my lover, what an atmosphere you create!
what talent you possess!
you are so convincing!
you understand the secret!
do you know how good you look!
what a luxury you are!
you are a gift of flesh and inspiration
an exotic angel that fell from heaven

I am self-indulgent!
I must plunge
within
the deep richness of this Venus
within
this abundance of pure, lush beauty!

CHOCOLETE SHE IS

Sable is your skin
    abundant is the vista of your scented palette
        bewitching is my journey

The flavor of your essence is that of a celebration
    its eternal taste lingers
        its sweet infection, that of dreams

Your persuasive passion has cast its spell on me
    I happily bathe within your auburn charm
        miracle of sweet milk chocolate

Stunning how this bronze wraps itself around me

GOSH

Oh!
you stood up
the sand clings to your body
you are wet from sweating
your thigh is a sculpture in grains of sand
Michelangelo couldn't have made anything more beautiful or more complete

the sand is not falling off as you walk toward the ocean

I am grinning
I find you so beautiful
you are art
you are nature
you are the sands of a million women
you are their femininity
their age
their understanding
their shyness
their bravado
you are the sun grasping the planets
you are the meaning of heaven on earth
and from the center of earth, you are gravity
keeping this world in flow and rhythm

Ah!
look at the way that sand clings to you!

THE BATH

we meet by an illuminating glow of candlelight most every night
our special rendezvous surrounds us in hot, healing water
we float in bliss
our time to caress and carry on
talk and touch
lather and laughs
it all becomes a passion play
we shampoo each other's hair
that feels so good!

we kiss
clean kisses
wet kisses
brilliant kisses
sweet spice of lust
we dry each other with soft towels
we are squeaky clean!
our evening is just beginning!

my siren, my treasure
standing by our bed
you are almost a dream
with your hair pulled back
skin shining
showing off your female instincts
nice and naughty
you are hypnotizing

you know what you do to me
divine creature
you flirt with me
and I make an attentive audience

let us seize the moment
play and persuade
tickle and tease
coax me
seduce me
squeeze me
hold on sweet and don't let go
let's get scorched silly by this exchange

ALLIGATOR

As if on stage, you stand there like a fiery Wild West Expose!
Loving every provoking moment
    You show off!

An eagle feather sweeps the band of your straw hat
Auburn curls cascade down,
    and reveal that cunning grin
    so sly, amid lips of rose
Self-assured, that look you express,
    so confident, possessed

Cowgirl naughty!
Wearing boots made from the skin of an alligator!

What an arousing invitation
Such, the masquerade
How well you pose!
With an open blouse of linen
    ah, those blue jeans, they vanished long ago
    just so you could flaunt your curves
      yes, such an attractive display of pleasure

You love to sashay in front of me
    so convincing, and so eager!
High-Heeled, twirling that lasso,
    you tease me with each sin that is coming next
    almost boasting about my ensuing treat

It's there, along the meadow
    The Land of Enchantment
    The Valley of Fire
      trance-like
      flourishing in sweet bliss
       so ripe for feasting
Your stunning dawn!
Your boundless release of heaven!
Have I told you, it's flawless!

Seductive Seamstress,
    You've carefully stitched each piece together
    Easily binding all that will float us off to Never-Never Land

You know, I bet you skinned that gator all by yourself!

THE SWEET SMILE ON YOUR FACE

my love
there is the sweetest smile on your face
you are so aroused
so alive
embracing your passion
embracing your beauty
I love seeing you this way

there is a wild look in your eyes
an eager savage touch as you lean into a kiss
your desires set free
your lush imagination
tempted
untamed
unlocked

dreamy rhythm conquest
your abundance of give and take
such delight in your exploration
such strength
such sensuality

surrendering to the woman within
you capture that sweet treasure
the joyous release
such a sacred sacrament of your power
the richness of your soaking celebration
magic in the banquet of your ecstasy

your spirit lifted
you glow in a saga of mysterious raw energy
your true nature set free

I respect how necessary this is for you
I honor that you share this wild gift with me

with that sweet smile on your face
you parade like Eve in the Garden of Eden
like Adam, I will eat anything you offer

MO

I love when you shout for more

    yes, I begin to soar

and if that's not enough

    you are most beautiful in the buff

WILD MOUNTAIN HONEY!

Like a queen bee
    you embody the essence of all women!

And from the hive of your primal gift to me…
      I lick, and I suck this creamy swollen richness!

Your satiated spark of feminine seduction,
    this enraged radiance,
      this blossom of plush elegant indulgence!

It's all so arousing!

So famished, and so eager
    I can't stop nourishing myself on your flower!

I've never tasted anything so erotic, and so satisfying!

LAVISH SOULS UNWIND

If only for this night
we shall soar across the universe
    silhouette to silhouette
    soul to soul

If only for this night
we shall rise above and let our hearts unite as one

You are so beautiful as you exalt to pristine heights
each angle of your essence revealed in a flood of senses
    its origin, like the beginning of an eager earth
        exposed and liberated
           enlightened

Itf only for this night
we shall awaken our spirits and together
    we will glide beyond all boundaries and discover new frontiers

I have no excuse but to be in love with you
      if only for this night

TREASURE

My Sweet Pleasure

We will press our bodies together

    and in elation,

        we will burn in the fury, and the glory of love

Only together

    within the days expanse,

        of midnights, untamed and true

            and in the deserted hours of morning

                we will uncover the path to the treasure

THE DANCE

Dear lady
you flirt with me
I am attracted,
  mesmerized,
    and so ready for all abandonment of logic
I surrender

Please, my sugary treat
  tell me,
I need to know, is this a game?
Does this mean anything to you?

Let's make it easy
If this is the latter,
I give up
I just won't go there
  such a waste of time
  such an invasion of my life joy

If this is seduction,
  let us move on to the next step
  let me kiss your neck
  explore the temptation of soft skin
    and even further,
      for more of your magic

And you,
   don't stop what you do so well
   go ahead
   amaze me

Let us become wild
  like animals,
   those that shriek and howl
     nudging
     biting and clawing
It's all part of this the wild game
     this encompassing aphrodisiac,
     nature's dance

Well dear
Shall we hold on to one another?
  kiss with satisfying hunger
if not,
wave good bye
I'm dancing out of here

DREAM-CATCHER

you keep a 'Dream-Catcher' in your window
I gaze at the colorful yarn of its geometric shape
    centuries of dreams
you said it works
    you dreamed me

once, your dreams were full of gallant men and sinful women
    many nights you were caressed and loved by them all
seductive twilight of the growing moon, I came to you in a deep dream
    I was a king dressed in velvet
        you were an empress in silk
            we danced in the clouds
then we were naked
    and I carried you to your bed

an early morning sun warms your bedroom
    subtle colors spread against the walls
a slight breeze blows through an open window
the 'Dream-Catcher' slowly twists in the wind
    I can see both sides of the dream

our love is like a dream
we time travel through it
    not quite awake
        catching a goodnights sleep in between dreams

BELLA

Bella, speak to me in the language of love

Let us drift into this mystic dream,

    and surround our dance with enchantment

Let's awake in the place of all shining magic

There, we will race free across the river stones

We shall soar within our sanctuary of tenderness

The way all colors collide

You and I will kiss the song of all searching hearts

We will inherit the heavens,

    embrace paradise together

Forever beyond this everlasting mystery

This truth has no option but to break loose

    and skyward,

        together,

            We shall fly!

KISS YOU TATTOO

in this moonlight

the two of you are fascinating

melody of a summer night

wrapped in that warm wind

    princess and princess

    woman caressing woman

smooth grace of desire

stargazing partners of a late night trance

      above the clouds

          shadow wind of the moment

midnight kisses in a tavern of urgency

divine union of honey-scented flesh

your smiles taunt and your eyes tease

you are offering me all of your sweetness

with such an intriguing invitation, I drift on this ocean of seductive sheets

this is such a tasteful language of loving

    all the gathering of senses and sins

as the candle's dripping dance lights our way,

    we celebrate in the depth of this fertile food

you do this so well!

      thorough
       innovative

       thieves of this dreamy story!

CRÈME DE LA CRÈME

There lies the sacred flower
    my senses ignite by its captivating aroma
        its exquisite taste
            oh, such a naughty, luscious tincture
              I so savor your treasure

Infinite woman that you are!

    I so cherish this voluptuous realm that you initiate!!

PASTRY

Such an impassioned celebration
    you arch and bend for my indulgence
        your taunting hourglass form illuminated
            and that stirring derriere poses so well
    only to applaud the pleasure of you
        there for my seizing

Oh this bakery window filled with delight
    suggesting the excessive tease
        yes I will
    please, please

EMPRESS WILD!

Empress,
   such a wild bounty of earth
You possess a mad appetite for loving
With that smile, and your feverish desire,
   you have hunted

My Tigress, you are circling your prey
   and now leap into my summer!
With no mercy, you lunge upon my universe!
Such, your longing for pleasure!

Sweet Venus,
I am so eager!
I long for the taste of your lips
I so ache to embrace each gem of your storm!

Oh, I am so anticipating this lustful celebration!
I am burning,
   Rock me!
     Shake me!
       Rock me!

Captured and overwhelmed,
   I am spinning from this excess!
The blood and breath of my being is devoured
All that was tangible in my life has now been engulfed in fire!

Here and now,
   consumed and contented,
   I've become a most satisfied victim

As in a dream, I prowl within a cave of intoxication
Lost in splendor
Staggering in your bewitched kingdom!

TIGRESS

lady

you have a dangerous and determined passion

like a tigress giving into temptation

    you stalk and circle your prey

        ravenous, you move in and seize your reward

this tigress will have her desire in her mouth

she won't stop until she and her delighted victim

    are lost in a dreamy state

lover

thank you for this beautiful bliss

FLAMES OF MYTHICAL MAGIC

Lover, it's so obvious
I'm only here as a diversion
Solely included to calm your appetite to be wicked
Just that, a blanket of flattery to entertain your desires
Recruited to deliver whatever is necessary to get you through the darkness
Is that it, just here to arouse you, Princess?

And I, in heated fury,
   eagerly volunteering to be the solution of your craving,
   attempting to calm your desperate need for affection,
   applauding your reckless appeasement to be ravaged,
   rejoicing in your remedy for loneliness,
only to recognize my own drunken desire to be saturated in love and lust!

I've become obsessed,
   no, even more,
      shackled, and crazed within these sweet flames of healing!
Wild inside this sphere of fiery magic!

     Bound in Enraged Flames of Mythical Magic!

SCULPTURE

Flush with the breath of night
we surrender to the eternal sky
our embrace floating on majestic wings of magic

So rich as marbled ghosts
   the tempest storm serenades the air of our midnight sculpture

All my journeys validated by the bouquet of your truth
   by the melody of your secret song
      your hair
        your glancing face
         your kiss
Oh to absorb the volume of your soul

Gladly, I breathe in your mystic magic
   ah yes, to breathe in your magic,
all the cyclone nights I have waited to be immersed within your arms

My carved empress, this night is ours

CURVES

Oh siren you sing a sweet sonnet
    it serenades my infection
        that dragon tattoo pleads my inspection

I must embrace the arch of your slender back
    taste each groove of your hide
        explore each sigh

Barefoot and drifting upon textured kisses
    our embrace and the boundaries become naked
        like the color of your skin at dawn
            ripe like tree fruit
                sweet, paved in honey

You, my siren, are a bundle of curves

SCHOLARS

for centuries
scholars
have attempted
to define heaven

I am tasting
the nectar
of your flower
you are gently
touching your breasts

your eyes are closed
you are moaning
and as you abandon all control
your head lifts up and back

your orgasm

this is heaven

CAPTURED

as the fever of your gypsy thighs rages on,

    my existence is seized in the pleasure of your fire

like the fury of an ocean wave rushing, and rising upon my life

    I tumble out of control from the surge

diving headfirst into this carousel of sweetened candy!

surrounded in this obsession of our nocturnal paradise,

    the eternal pulse of love commands my soul

EXPLOSION IN HEAVEN!

to be in your body

moving

sliding

through the gates of heaven

within the garden of a Goddess

I crave for this gift!

sweetheart

you look fresh, fabulous and on fire

you are squirming in delight

you are about to explode

lover, violently erupt all over me

I want to feel it fully

I love it!

SORCERY

the lake of your love appears luminous
it's surface is a tranquil mirror of watercolors
graceful, gentle ripples wave a friendly hello
leaves in the shallows adorn in delicate design on your skin
morning reflections tenderly grace the garden of your essence

in the quiet of the night
    the very quiet
in the soft stillness of the nocturnal
you are here, my treasure
you lie in the bliss of slumber
your breath relaxed
eyes of blue, lost in a dream
sleep now my love
we will reach out to one another at the dawning of a new day

the seduction of my heart, and this wild exploration of all that you are
I must consume the creamy bliss of your body
savor your skin
    soft as silk
travel legs of forever
kiss
    perfectly
        painted
            pink toes

my lover
my sweet lady
your alluring magic
your sorcery
    has me deep in the rapture of this ecstasy!

AUTUMN

Your Autumn legs surround me
Oh, the sweetness of this encompassing embrace

My Treasure,
Now is our season of trance
A festival of two hearts
    held tight
    sharing the world, wherever our world

Your skilled Autumn legs of love
    calming my ache for a mirror image
    awakening the lingering sunrise of my longing
    and after, to escort an inspired heartbeat

A banquet of morning secrets abound by Autumn legs
They launch a delicate yearning
    only to slowly cascade down upon the shore of your mystic horizon

Autumn Elegance
Bend your life over my chest
Sing the diamonds clear
Fortunes gather like emeralds across your skin
    browned by radiance
    sun swept pollen

Graceful, ripened legs of Autumn

Indian Summer of Autumn!

THE DAWN OF VENUS

Here, in the air of thunder,
    we unlock a sunrise of temptation
In this theater of passion,
    your Savanna lipstick serenades my life
And from behind a gentle veil, your Venus aura arises

Oh My Tigress, I love our lustful ballet
Our surrender to the sweet urgency of want
Our rendezvous of silk and senses!

The heights we aspire too!
Our plunge into the bonfire of flesh thievery!
There will be no end to this pageant of love!

An infinite sky will open
    Heaven will shake
        Our palace will be inflamed!

This will be the ledge we are meant to fall from
And we shall fall into contented soothing oblivion
This is where we replenish the heartbeat of life!

Standing mythically proud, like Mars,
    I will be the fire rhapsody that unlocks the origin of Venus

TWIRLING

there is a woman dancing around my bedroom
she sways so free
it is mesmerizing to behold her wild storm

she rotates in multi-colors
her twirling makes me dizzy

a woman dancing, is there anything more beautiful?

I think I will join her on the dance floor

COFFEE SHOP MORNING #4

Hours later, and I still can smell your scent upon my skin
provoked with by such intensity,
    our love becomes saturated in the sensual fragrance

Stunning how our inflamed embrace melts our spirits together
    it's intoxicating

Siren, blend your harmonies across my life
    your song is soothing
        its melody fills the skies
            and encircles my heart with the vast expanse of your beauty

oh sweetness,
the day's length, and to be here with you
the naked rhythm creating such naughty rhymes
it's a pool of passion

I extend my soul by sharing these stanzas
    meant for eyes of my lover
I am a poet
    and I shall compose lyrics that sing of the sinful sugar you possess

Coffee shop morning, and my friends wonder why I am grinning so

EARTH FLOWER

At the dawning, the crescent moon began to slowly fade
    giving way to the birth of day
The morning's glow, ever so faint,
   gently teased,
    the darkness had no choice but to surrender its grasp
My true direction appeared in these early hours

I navigated a lonely prairie that soon gave way to a pathway
   hidden from most,
    those who would not be searching
A clearing emerged,
   and there, a shining of pearls and jade arose

I ensued deeper, and about me, a mysterious garden appeared
I did not recognize this kingdom
My footsteps led me upon an intriguing flower
A Wild Rose was its companion, as was an Orchid

This blossom was so unique,
   its rapture, pristine in nature,
    appearing to be cultivated by some divine essence

I knelt, inspecting the delicate bud
Its lips, plump and blooming, flaunted fantasy
I discovered its mystic petals, violet and pink, were flush with fragrance
Exotic whites fluttered in harmony at its center
Here, each subtle hue flourished in luminous clusters of invitation

Charmed and mesmerized, as if under a hypnotic spell,
   I felt as if I commenced to rise above the mundane world
   I began to ascend to a more noble persuasion,
     one of truth and sincerity

I realized, I could never abandon this flower
This gallant gift, guide and ally,
   this friend and companion,
     This Woman

Given a wiser path, one of fulfillment
My searching ceased,
    I embraced life anew!

ASIA

A delicate silk sarong
   falls with envy over your jeweled hips
Movement enhances the pleasure of seeing you glide toward me
Graceful
  like the jade of your reclusive necklace
just so, hidden from its radiance
  to blossom and rage like the exotic flower that you are

Mystic Princess,
Escape with me
We will journey to the far horizon
  for this parade of night
  for this longing, and the fire

Distant mountains only dream of your shadow
Your hand print has pierced my heart
  heart of hearts

I awake in the honeyed valleys of your body
  celebrating the festival of you
Kiss me,
  let your lips brush the substance of my enchantment
Unearth the mosaic of my abduction

Like naked poetry
  dancing
My treasure, I abandon all for our embrace
Always Asia

YOUR DEFINING NECK

I could write lines of alluring verse about your lovely face

it would be easy to accommodate the pages with entertaining pleasure

all the approving meaningful sensuous positions you wear yourself

I would not have to coax the words to illuminate the way you persuade

but I want to focus on your neck

the way it dares to be kissed

the way it initiates caresses

your lustful neck

and the feeling I get when my lips applaud its skin

when I stand near you, I just as soon lift your head this way and that

so to get at all the daring angles of your convincing influence

your sensuality expands itself through that exquisite neck

my exploration has to be thorough

I have to be sure my kiss settles just where you desire it

this pleases you and a smile appears on your lips

at twilight your neck settles elegantly like poetry

at daybreak it rests gracefully like a Rodin sculpture

defining

mesmerizing

captivating

WOMAN

this moment of intrigue
    this spell of love
these innocent and gallant emotions
you and I both held captive
    both set free

in a simple instant we aroused an appetite for romance
    emotions awoke from slumber
    a new frontier expanded in colors

the sphere of our love
    reason enough
    not to discover the boundary

sweet enchanter
    you have made me
    wanted and needed
    bold and strong
    alive

you have ignited a flame that heats my heart,
    and melts my soul

I've come along for this ride
I abandon memories of past lovers
women with their soothing, eternal scent
    replaced and rewarded
    with a new woman's fragrance
    your fragrance

I can not seem to get enough
your smile says it's not enough
    so take Lorenzo
    and I take
    I want
    I feast

I won't be satisfied with a moment
I need a season of you
I want your bouquet
    to fill my house
    to fill my time
    to fill my life

TURQUOISE KISS

Turquoise
Blue stone of ancient fables
how it hangs from your body
It glorifies you

The embrace
The one that took me by surprise
hypnotic as the eternal sky
Turquoise evermore

Kiss me once
  and again, once more
Drench me in a shower of wonders
My passage, filled with rushing rivers of passion
  carry me, and plunge my emotions from shore to shore
  to the shore of the infinite

River boulders of self
  lodged for decades
  hidden from expressing the longing
flattered and released
liberated
boundless
    limitless

My Jewel,
So vivid, so revealing
I rest on the warm side of your shadow
I worship in the light of your smile

Exhausted,
  exposed and exalted
I awake within this turquoise indulgence

Turquoise Evermore

SYRENS

They are everywhere,

   clustered among waves and shores, ponds and gardens

Graciously strolling through meadows, and our minds

Cleverly handing out a shimmering of hope and happiness

They call with seductive whispers from heaven

   daring us to join their dance

We echo our response,

   and swim out to sea whatever the danger,

   how ever sharp the dagger

Embracing what we most desire,

   The magic!

TO SING

It's fine if you believe in reincarnation,

    I respect your space

I don't believe in reincarnation,

    but just in case,

    and I am reborn again,

    and as a man,

I desire to come back with an impressive voice

    one with tone and resonance,

    one with machismo!

I want to sing love songs to women

JAZZ

The sway you swing is so persuading
    for eternities, you are the convincing sorcerous
spreading your hypnotic essence aloft
    you encourage the mystic dance so well

Oh my muse, I am gliding within this fantasy
    here, I can celebrate heaven

This must be the bright horizon I've heard so much about

MAGIC OF THE MUSE

I've seen her sleek shadow
I have witnessed her magic arising like a fable

I've held her so near, grasping the golden warmth of her embrace
    the fields of rapture, free within my soul

Do you see how she dances and twirls
    swaying so beneath the full moon
        arousing the harvest!

The muse sings the elusive melody
Do you hear her siren's song beckoning?

> *Dressed in summer white,*
> *parading in the warm light,*
> *and for all the heaven of this night*
> *the muse begins to dance*
> *my first glance*
> *Oh the spell, the trance*

> *Wild with passion*
> *she dusts the meadow in fine lace*
> *enhancing the haunting with such grace*

Oh to unearth a storm so sacred!
Muse, you are to be consumed by savage and reckless poets!

Made in the USA
Columbia, SC
20 May 2021